ROBERT CHURCHWELL:
WRITING NEWS, MAKING HISTORY

A SAVANNAH GREEN STORY

ROBERT CHURCHWELL:
WRITING NEWS, MAKING HISTORY

A SAVANNAH GREEN STORY

BY
GLORIA
RESPRESS-
CHURCHWELL

ILLUSTRATED BY
MICHAEL
MCBRIDE

Jabberwocky Press,
Minneapolis

To my inspirational mother, Doris Respress, and Mary Churchwell, who showed how dignity could walk alongside adversity.
Eternally grateful, Gloria

Jabberwocky Press
322 First Avenue N, 5th floor
Minneapolis, MN 55401
612.455.2293
www.Jabberwocky-Books.com

Jabberwocky
Books

ISBN-13: 978-1-63413-059-2
LCCN: 2014949889

Distributed by Itasca Books

Illustrations by Michael J. McBride
Images from Churchwell Mural by artists Michael J. McBride and James R. Threalkill
Graphics of Mural by Daniel Breton
Cover Design by Mary Kristin Ross
Typeset by James Arneson

Printed in the United States of America

As the school bus eased to a stop, Savannah Green quickly grabbed her backpack and ran to her new home. Her mother waited eagerly at the front door, biting her bottom lip. She was excited to hear about her daughter's first day in third grade at her new school, Robert Churchwell Elementary.

Before her mother could greet her, Savannah blurted out, "Mom, I hate that school! I want to be back at my old school with my friends! I don't want to be here!"

Savannah's mom smiled sadly. "Savannah, I know this is all new to you, but with time you'll grow to love your new school and make new friends."

"My real friends are in Chicago! I hate that dumb school! I'll never love that school!" Savannah shouted angrily. She stomped into the living room and threw her backpack on the floor, flinging herself on the sofa and squeezing her favorite pillow to her chest. Her life felt like a mess. She wished her dad could make it all better like he used to.

Clutching her pillow even tighter, Savannah remembered that rainy night in Chicago three months ago. Her dad was driving home from work. A truck slid and crashed into his car. He died in the ambulance on the way to the hospital. Savannah didn't get to say goodbye to her dad, and her heart was broken. Her mother was heartbroken too.

After her husband's death, Savannah's mom made the hard decision to move to Nashville, Tennessee, to be closer to family. Savannah knew her father would want them to be around relatives, but she missed her old life—her old neighborhood, her old school, and her old friends. Most of all, she missed her daddy. Savannah tried to believe that things would get better. Like her dad used to say, "Running begins with a single step." But Savannah could only think about the sadness and grief that burned her throat.

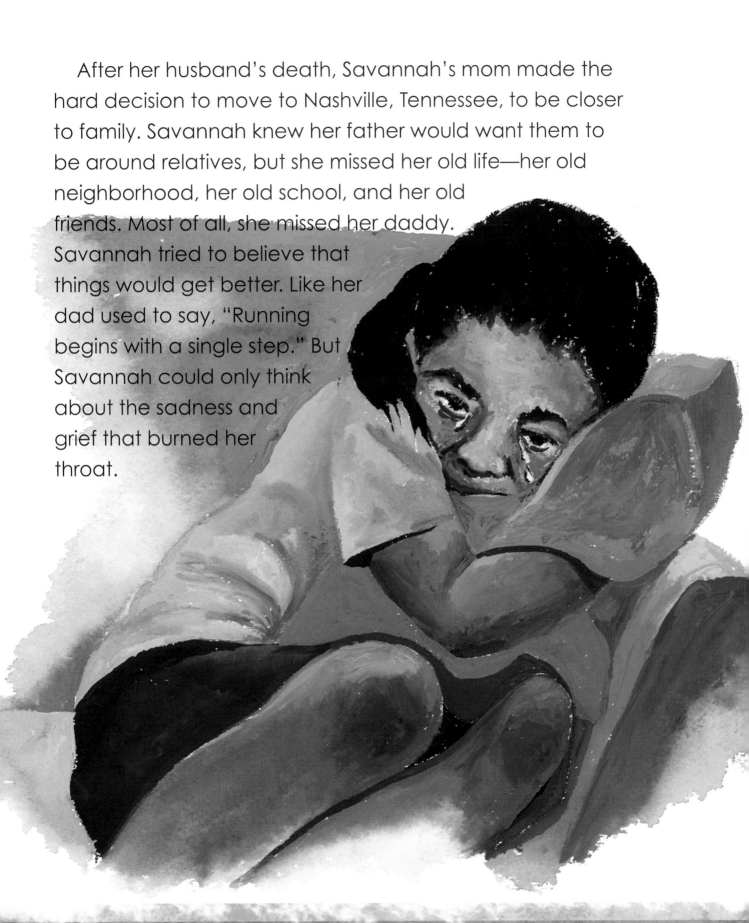

"Sweetie, it'll be okay. With time, you'll see, things will get better," her mom said quietly. She walked over to her daughter's backpack and pointed to a poster sticking out of it. "Savannah, what's this?"

Savannah's mother pulled the poster out and stared at the collage of pictures.

Savannah raised her head from her pillow and rushed over to her mother. She snatched the poster out of her mom's hands and ripped it to pieces. "It's a stupid poster about the man that stupid school is going to celebrate tomorrow."

"Honey, I know you're not mad about a poster," Savannah's mom said gently, resting her hands on Savannah's shoulders. "I know you miss Daddy just as much as I do. I never thought he wouldn't be here with us today, or that we would ever leave Chicago."

Savannah began to cry, and her mother held her tightly. "Sweetheart, that car accident may have taken your dad, but it can't take any of our memories. I know if your dad were here today, he would want me to share an important story with you."

"You see, Savannah," her mother said as she kneeled down and began matching the torn poster pieces together on the hardwood floor, "your dad knew Robert Churchwell, the man your school is named after. When your father went to college, Mr. Churchwell was his mentor."

"He was?" Savannah asked, scooting closer to her mother while drying her eyes. "Did you know him, Mom?"

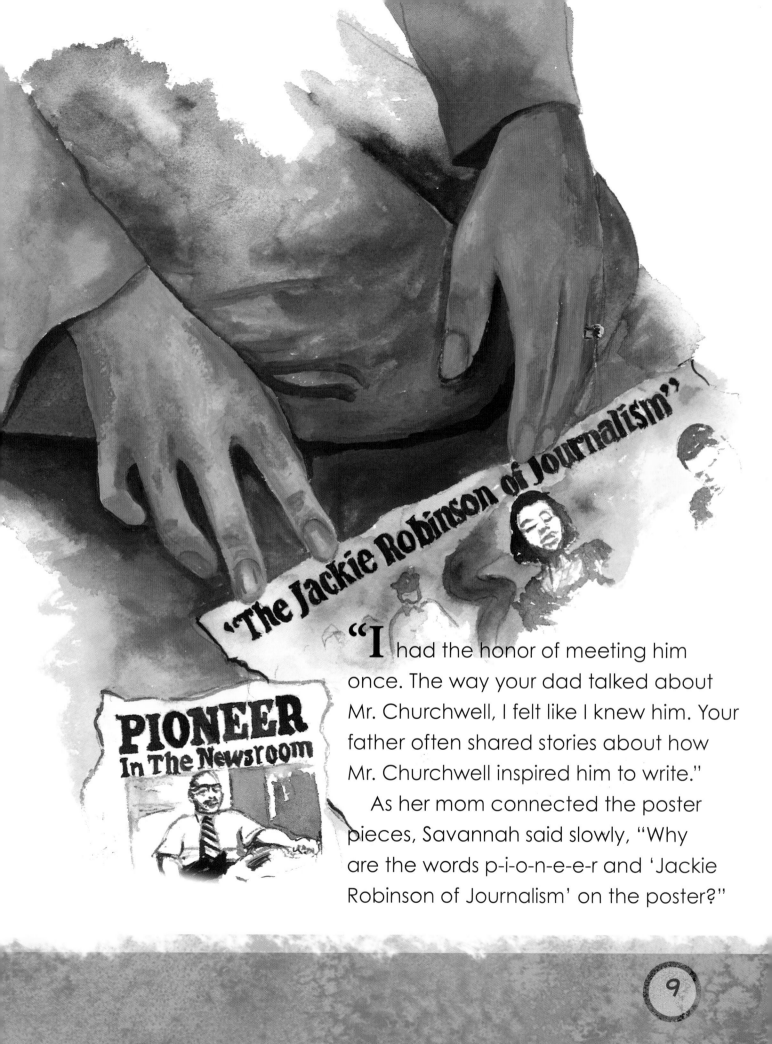

"The Jackie Robinson of Journalism"

PIONEER
In The Newsroom

"I had the honor of meeting him once. The way your dad talked about Mr. Churchwell, I felt like I knew him. Your father often shared stories about how Mr. Churchwell inspired him to write."

As her mom connected the poster pieces, Savannah said slowly, "Why are the words p-i-o-n-e-e-r and 'Jackie Robinson of Journalism' on the poster?"

"A pioneer is anyone who is the first to do something, Savannah," her mom answered.

"What does 'Jackie Robinson of Journalism' mean?" Savannah asked.

"During the 1950s," her mother explained, "the *Nashville Banner*—one of the two all-white city newspapers in Nashville—was looking for an African American writer whose work would encourage more African Americans to buy their newspaper. At the time, newspapers in the South like the *Banner* didn't have any African American journalists."

Savannah continued to look at the words as her mom continued.

"Robert Churchwell was thought to be the best man for the job because he was known for writing positive stories about African Americans in a community newspaper he and a friend had created. At first, Robert Churchwell refused to write for the *Banner* because the newspaper didn't respect African Americans. The paper was known for writing stories about blacks not being as smart as whites."

"Why did Mr. Churchwell change his mind?" Savannah asked.

"Well, Savannah, Robert Churchwell finally agreed to work for the newspaper because his wife and friends convinced him that being a journalist for the paper was important. They knew that he would be the first African American to work for a major daily newspaper in the South. They told him that he would be a pioneer, the 'Jackie Robinson of Journalism.' Robert Churchwell was a journalism pioneer."

"But Mom," Savannah said, puzzled, "what does that have to do with Jackie Robinson?"

"Jackie Robinson was a baseball player and he was a pioneer too," Savannah's mom explained.

"He was the first person to play baseball?" Savannah asked.

"No," said her mother, "he was the first African American to play professional baseball with white players in the major leagues."

"Well, who did he play with before that?" Savannah asked.

"He played in the all-black Negro baseball league," her mom responded. "Back then, especially in the South, not only were blacks and whites segregated at work, which means they worked apart, blacks together and whites together, but they were also segregated when playing sports."

"How was Mr. Churchwell related to Mr. Robinson?" Savannah questioned.

"In 1947, Jackie Robinson became the first black man to play for the Brooklyn Dodgers, a major league baseball team. In 1950, Robert Churchwell became the first black man to work as a journalist at the *Nashville Banner*. Early on, people compared Robert Churchwell to Jackie Robinson. That's why he is known as the 'Jackie Robinson of Journalism.'"

Savannah sat up as she made the connection. "Mommy, remember when Daddy worked at the *Chicago Tribune?* All races worked together, and when we went to baseball games with Daddy, we always saw people of different races playing together."

"That's right, Savannah," her mother said, planting a kiss on Savannah's forehead. "Robert Churchwell and Jackie Robinson helped make those opportunities possible."

Savannah stared at the poster again.

"Mom," she said with a serious face, "what is happening in this picture of the little girls and the policeman? She looks like that girl named after a birthstone, Ruby."

"That's right, Savannah, she does look like Ruby Bridges. Where did you learn about her?"

"I learned about her at my old school. She was one of the first African American students to go to an all-white school in New Orleans, where Dad's favorite team, the Saints, play. She was in the first grade. The police had to protect her from mean people," Savannah answered.

"Good memory, sweetie! This picture represents what it was like for black children like Ruby Bridges to attend school with white children for the first time. It shows little girls being protected by the police on their way to school because some people didn't want 'integration,' which means that black children and white children would go to the same school."

"Mom, my teacher, Ms. Upshaw, picked Suni to be my room buddy. I told her about Dad's accident and about you and me being new to Nashville. Suni told me that her grandparents are from India."

"**I**'m happy that you met a new friend, Savannah. It's nice that you go to a school with students from different cultures. At one time, segregation made it hard for blacks and whites to do things together. That's why it was so important that Jackie Robinson and Robert Churchwell played and worked with white people. They challenged segregation."

"That's so brave, Mommy."

"Yes, it is. Blacks and whites worked together to change the law. This effort was known as the civil rights movement," her mom shared. "Robert Churchwell wrote about what was going on at that time. He wrote stories about the unfair things that were happening to African Americans and how people like Dr. Martin Luther King, Jr., were changing our country for the better."

Savannah pointed to the poster with a big smile. "Oh! There's Dr. King."

"Robert Churchwell met many famous people like Dr. King. And look, there is Muhammad Ali, the boxer, and Marian Anderson. She was a famous opera singer and one of the first African Americans to sing at the White House."

"Wow, she sang at the White House just like Beyoncé!" Savannah beamed.

Her mom, catching Savannah's smile, said, "Yes, she did, honey. Savannah, Robert Churchwell grew up during segregation when it was legal to have whites and blacks go to separate schools and parks, and use different bathrooms and water fountains."

"Did segregation start before Ruby Bridges was born, Mom?"

"Yes, it did. It began even before Mr. Churchwell was born. It started when a man named Homer Plessy took a stand. Have you ever heard of Homer Plessy?" her mother asked.

Savannah shook her head no.

"Well, he was a shoemaker of African and French descent," her mom continued. "His skin color was very light, making him look white. In 1892, he was arrested for riding in a 'whites only' train car in Louisiana on the East Louisiana Railroad. Homer Plessy was put in jail for breaking the law that forbid any person with black ancestors from sitting in any area other than the 'colored' or 'black' section of the train car. Train cars for black passengers were not as nice as the cars for white travelers."

"That's wrong, Mommy."

"That's right, Savannah. Plessy went to court because he too believed that as an American citizen he deserved the right to travel in safe, clean transportation. Plessy tried to change unfair things that were happening to African Americans."

"Mr. Plessy won his case, right, Mom? After all, he was an American citizen," Savannah said, leaning toward her mother with her elbows on her knees.

"No, honey, he lost. The Supreme Court ruled in 1896 that segregation was okay as long as everything was 'separate but equal' for blacks and whites. Although Mr. Plessy lost," Savannah's mom said, "he helped in making things better for African Americans."

"How, Mom?"

"Well, in 1954, over sixty years after Homer Plessy took his stand, big changes began to happen. The Supreme Court decided in a case called *Brown v. Board of Education* that separating black and white students was against the law."

"That's good, Mommy! Mr. Plessy really started something. It's like what Dad used to say: "Running begins with a single step."

Savannah's mom pulled her closer. She matched the torn pieces featuring Robert Churchwell reading to a circle of children.

Savannah pointed to one of the students in the picture who was seated in the circle and said, "She looks like Emily, one of Suni's friends. She showed me an easy way to draw animals in art class today."

"**A**re those kids in the circle students in Mr. Churchwell's class?" Savannah asked.

"No, Savannah, Mr. Churchwell wasn't a school teacher, but schools often invited him to read to their students. Many people in the public schools knew Mr. Churchwell. During his years at the newspaper, he wrote important stories about black children going to school with white children," her mom explained.

"Oh! Mr. Churchwell wrote about i-n-t-e-g-r-a-t-i-o-n," Savannah said, pronouncing the word perfectly.

Savannah's mom chuckled. "Like your dad always said, you are one smart young lady."

"Mommy, what did Daddy like most about Mr. Churchwell?" Savannah asked, as her hands gripped her knees.

"I would say . . ." Her mom paused. "His humble beginnings. He was born in a small town in Tennessee called Clifton."

"The name of that town is on the poster," Savannah said as she pointed to the words *Clifton, Tennessee*.

"He and his sister and three brothers grew up here, in Nashville," her mother said. "He was a child during the Great Depression, a difficult time in America when many people were without jobs. His family was extremely poor, and no matter the weather, Mr. Churchwell walked long distances to and from school in shoes that were lined with pieces of cardboard. His parents couldn't afford to buy him new clothes or shoes and he even sold bones to help feed his family."

"How?" Savannah asked.

"As a little boy," her mom answered, "Mr. Churchwell collected bones from trash cans. The bones were used to make soap."

Savannah gasped. "Bones were used to make soap?"

"Yes, Savannah, but despite his hardships, Mr. Churchwell always enjoyed writing stories about the world around him. After high school, Robert Churchwell served in the United States Army and fought in World War II," her mom said.

"Did he write in the Army?" Savannah asked.

"He often wrote letters to the Army leaders about the poor conditions of African Americans in the military," her mom said. "Their barracks were not as nice as the white soldiers' barracks, and at times, the African American soldiers were served cold food."

"Did he go to college?" Savannah asked.

Before her mother could answer, Savannah remembered seeing the words Fisk University on the poster.

"Don't tell me, Mom. He went to Fisk like Daddy. Wow! I bet he was really, really smart."

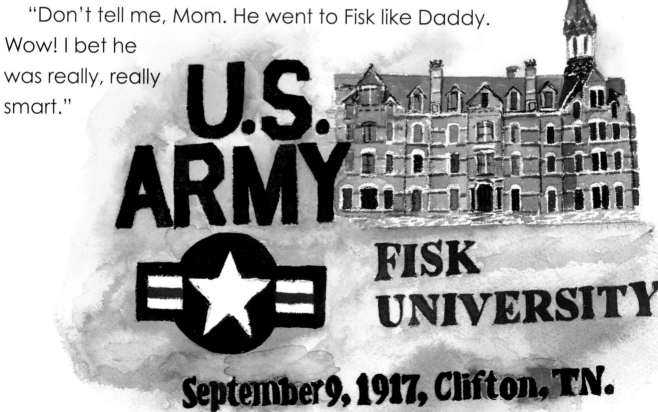

U.S. ARMY

FISK UNIVERSITY

September 9, 1917, Clifton, TN.

Savannah's mom nodded. "He did go to Fisk after serving in the war. But, there was a time when Mr. Churchwell doubted his ability to learn. He was teased in school for not being smart. His mother always made him feel good about his writing talent. She never called him dumb like some people at his school did."

"That's mean, Mommy," Savannah said, pouting her lips. "That's name-calling and name-calling is bullying."

"Yes, name-calling is bullying," her mom agreed. "Robert Churchwell was bullied. But he didn't let other people's views shape how he saw himself. Two things that kept him going were his belief that he could write good stories and his mother's confidence in him that he would do great things.

Mr. Churchwell was very determined to do something with his life, despite his challenges."

Wanting to know more about the man her father admired, Savannah asked, "Mom, did Mr. Churchwell have children?"

Her mother nodded. "Yes, Savannah, he did. After graduating from Fisk, Robert Churchwell met Mary Buckingham, an elementary school teacher. They married and raised five children."

"Who's this with Mr. Churchwell, Mom?" Savannah pointed to the image of a man pinning something on Robert Churchwell.

"That is a man named Dr. R. H. Boyd. He owns a publishing company that Mr. Churchwell worked at after he retired from the *Nashville Banner*," her mom said.

"Why didn't Mr. Churchwell just rest after working at the newspaper?" Savannah asked.

Her mother thought for a moment before responding. "Savannah, you know how Daddy enjoyed writing stories and reading them to you on his days off?"

"Yes, Mommy, I loved Daddy's stories!"

"Writing made your dad happy. Like Daddy, Robert Churchwell loved to write. And sweetie, you should always do what makes you smile inside."

"What did Mr. Churchwell get for all that writing?"

"Robert Churchwell received many awards, and his articles are included in the Smithsonian National Museum of African American History and Culture in Washington, DC."

"That's a really important museum," Savannah added. "Mom, what do you think made Mr. Churchwell the happiest?"

"That's a great question, Savannah. Your dad always said that Mr. Churchwell was most proud when he talked about his wife and five children. Two became teachers and three became doctors."

"Ohhh, there's Mr. Churchwell's nice family," Savannah said, pointing at the poster.

Her mom replaced the last piece and Savannah stared at the images before her.

"You know what, Mom?" Savannah said as her brown eyes sparkled.

"What's that, honey?"

"My school is special because it's named after a really good man, a man who taught Daddy and me how to be better." Savannah gave her mom a gigantic hug.

The next day the students at Robert Churchwell Elementary celebrated Robert Churchwell Day. During class, Savannah's teacher, Ms. Upshaw, asked, "Who can tell me why Robert Churchwell is known as the 'Jackie Robinson of Journalism?'"

Savannah eagerly waved her hand while bouncing up and down behind her desk. "Oh! I know! I know! Ms. Upshaw!"

"Okay, Savannah, tell us why Robert Churchwell is known as the 'Jackie Robinson of Journalism.'"

Suni and Emily sat next to Savannah and smiled brightly as their friend stood and spoke in a loud voice. "Robert Churchwell was the first African American to work at an all-white newspaper that was called the *Nashville Banner*. And Mr. Robinson was the first African American to play baseball for an all-white team in the major leagues. So they were both pioneers."

"Good answer, Savannah," Ms. Upshaw said.

Savannah grinned. *Running begins with a single step*. She was beginning to really love her new school.

Author's Note

"Don't give up!"

"You can do it!"

"Keep it up!"

These are sayings that motivate us to reach inside and do our very best. They are also words Robert Churchwell used to inspire everyone he knew. When I first met Robert Churchwell, I knew he was special. After becoming his daughter-in-law, I learned more about his fascinating story.

He was born in Clifton, TN, in 1917. His family was poor, segregation was a way of life, and he had few choices for making a living. Despite these challenges, Churchwell used his determination and the gift of writing to make history as the first African American to work at the *Nashville Banner*, a major daily newspaper in the South.

Early on I didn't understand why my father-in-law didn't freely share information about what it was like to work at the newspaper. I took for granted that being a journalism pioneer at an all-white newspaper was a significant milestone that should be shared to inspire others, especially children. But I was told an important message by Mary Churchwell, his wife of fifty-seven years and my mother-in-law: "Being the first is never easy."

Savannah Green, a fictional third grader, was created to introduce Robert Churchwell's motivational narrative to children. Stories told through her eyes help students celebrate unsung heroes like Robert Churchwell, a pioneer whose contribution to history helped make our society great!

—Gloria Respress-Churchwell

Index